By Kelly Chapman

Art by Faith Beckloff

Princess
with a
Purpose

Holy to the Lord

For my precious Kendall,

and all girls who want to know how to become a real princess.

Text © 2006 Kelly Chapman
Illustration © 2006 Faith Beckloff

Published by Princess with a Purpose, P.O. Box 55449 Houston, Texas 77255

Printed in the United States of America.
ISBN 0-9779093-0-1 SAN 850-4644

Once upon a real time,
there lived an eight-year-old girl
named Caroline who loved everything princess.
In her heart she dreamed of one day becoming
a real princess, but in her mind
she knew it was only make-believe.

Or was it?

"This is the day; this is the day that
the Lord has made. Wake up my jewel; wake up my jewel.
It's time for princess school," sang Caroline's grandmother.

"Oh Ge-Ge, you don't have to wake me up!" said Caroline. "I'm ready to
start the second most favorite day of my whole life! I can't wait to learn how
to be a real princess at Princess Prep School. But do you know what my first most
favorite day is? It's the day Jesus came to live in my heart. Remember that day,
Ge-Ge? You helped me pray to ask Jesus into my heart."

"I do remember," said Ge-Ge, "because it's also my most favorite day.
Now let's hurry so you're not late to start your second most favorite day."

"Hey! You can't start your day without me!" cried Kendall,
Caroline's talkative four-year-old sister. Kendall loved everything
that Caroline loved. "I'll be ready to start my second most
favorite day," she added, "just as soon as Caroline picks
out what we're, I mean, she's going to wear."

As the girls hurried to get ready, Caroline wished she and Kendall could arrive at Princess Prep School in a horse-drawn carriage. She wished they also had a king as a father and a queen as a mother so they could be real princesses. But in reality, all she and Kendall had was an ordinary car and Ge-Ge. They had lived with her ever since they could remember.

The ride to school was short. But as Caroline and Kendall walked to the classroom, Caroline began to feel uneasy. Would she really fit in? Could she ever be a real princess? With a sigh, Caroline slightly opened the door and saw something that took her breath away. It was the most amazing trunk she had ever seen. Standing next to the trunk was a lady who looked like an angel. Caroline watched as she opened the trunk and pulled out the most beautiful princess dresses. In fact, she saw one that sparkled like a pink diamond. But then, the classroom door flew open. Right in front of her stood…

Princess
Prep School

"How great is the love the Father has lavished on us, that we should be called children of God!" I John 3:1

"What are you-u-u doing here?" asked Prissy Crissy. "You know, to be a real princess you have to have a king as your father and a queen as your mother."

"Yea, Caroline, where's your mommy? Where's your daddy?" asked Missy, Prissy Crissy's best friend.

"Hey, don't be mean!" said Kimmy, Caroline's best friend. "She has a right to be here, too!"

Before Caroline could say anything, the lady spoke. "I'm so glad you're here, Caroline. My name is Miss Lily. I'm your Princess Prep School teacher. I'd like to show you the Trunk of Treasures. I'm quite sure you'll find something special in it just for you."

The girls gathered around Miss Lily. She began to teach them what it means to be a real princess. They all listened carefully, except Caroline. She looked rather unhappy. She didn't feel very "princessy" even though she was dressed like one. She thought about how all the other girls had a mommy and a daddy to go home to. But she and Kendall did not. This wasn't turning out to be her second most favorite day after all. In fact, she couldn't wait until it was over!

That night at home, Caroline decided to go to bed early. As she lay in bed, she began to pray. "Jesus, I love my Ge-Ge, but I need a mommy and a daddy to be a real princess." She cried until her eyes closed. And then she began to dream a dreamy kind of dream where the skies were bluer, the pinks were pinker, and the castles, well, the castles were heavenly...

She dreamed she was at Princess Prep School dressed in her beautiful princess gown with Kendall and all their friends.

Suddenly, the King's helper entered the room. His name was Constant because he was constantly forgetting things. And he always spoke in rhyme. He had come to invite the girls to a royal tea party at the Castle of Calvary.

Scratching his head Constant mumbled,
"Oh where! Oh where, did I put the royal invitation?
Oh dear! Oh me! Without it there'll be no proclamation!"

"Are you looking for this?" asked Kendall, holding up a royal scroll.

"Oh, yes! Yes! Yes! How very kind!
And it's just in the nick of time!"
exclaimed Constant, as he continued.

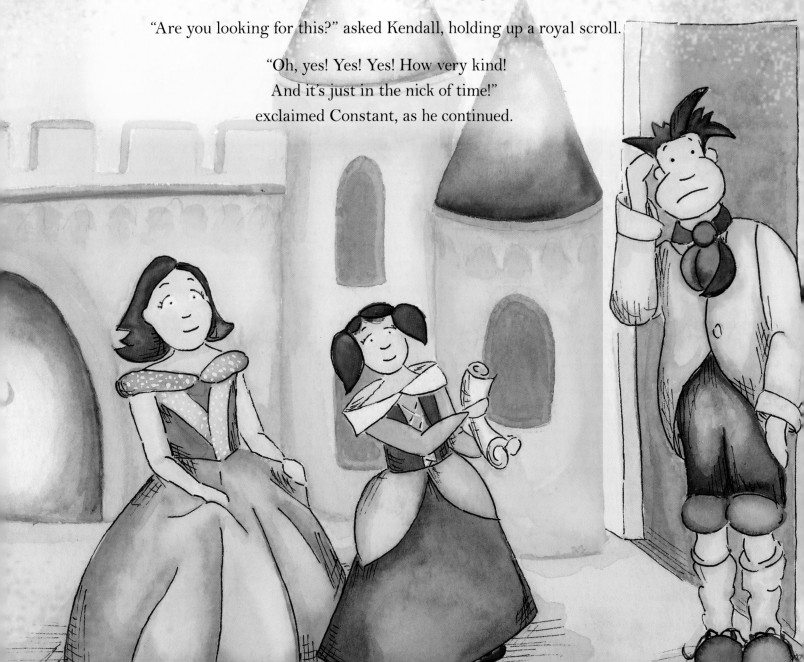

As Constant finished reading the invitation, a beautiful horse-drawn carriage came to take the girls to the castle. They could hardly believe their eyes. All of them jumped up and down with excitement! They were going to a real tea party to meet a real princess in a real carriage!

"Me first!" demanded Prissy Crissy.
She pushed her way to the front of the line.
"My mommy and daddy must have planned this. I'm sure it's
a surprise for my birthday. I told them I wanted a party with
everything pretty and pink and princess!"

Caroline was the last to enter the carriage.
Her heart sank as she saw there were no more seats.

"Sorry Caroline! I guess there's only room for real princesses,"
said Prissy Crissy with a laugh.

But Constant came to her rescue.
"Oh skittle dee dee! Now, now, let me see," said Constant.
"I have a special place for you.
Right up front, where there's room for two."
He bowed and continued,
"Constant is my name. Serving is my aim.
I am the King's attendant. And this day is sure to be splendid.
Caroline, won't you sit up front with me?
That way you'll be the first to see
the Castle of Calvary."

"Yee-haw! What a beautiful day it is for a tea party!"
said a friendly, country voice.

"Who…who…who said that?" asked Caroline.

"Is it true? Did I forget to introduce you two?"
asked Constant. "Caroline, meet Keydon, the King's royal horse.
His job is to keep us running on course."

"A ta-ta-talkking horse?" stuttered Caroline.

"Of course, it's a horse. It's Keydon, the talking horse.
He's wise, he's kind, and always on time.
Oh, and he's also a friend of mine!" said Constant.

"I'm pleased to meet you Caroline," said Keydon. "I'm glad you sat
up front, too. That way I can tell you about the Prince of Calvary."

As they traveled up the road, Keydon told His story. Caroline
listened to every word about the Prince's sacrifice for His royal
subjects. As Keydon finished, the carriage pulled up to the castle.

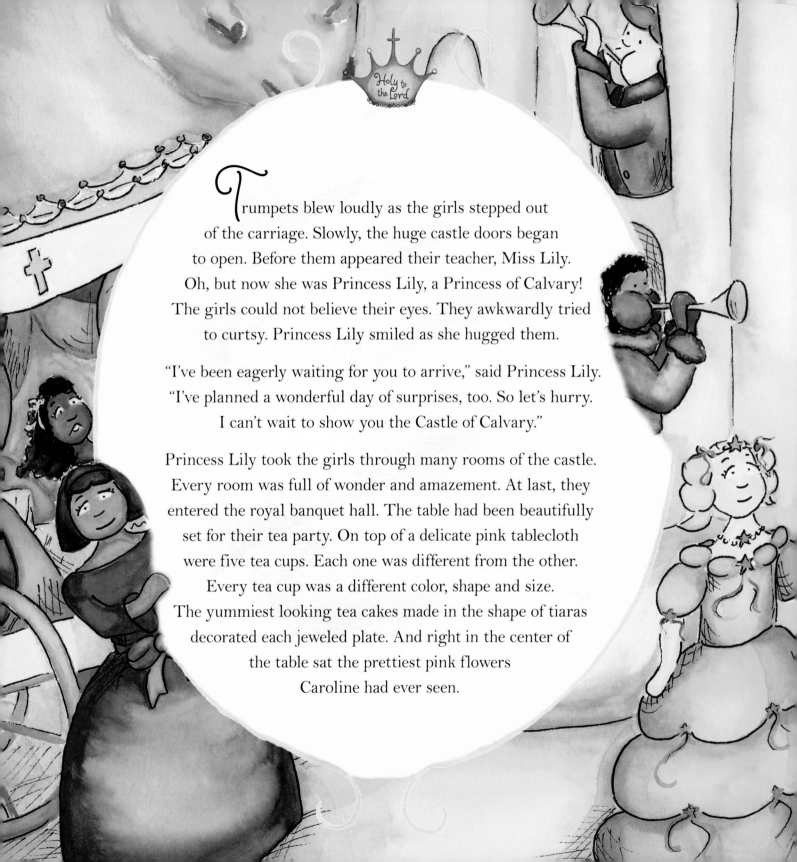

Holy to
the Lord

Trumpets blew loudly as the girls stepped out
of the carriage. Slowly, the huge castle doors began
to open. Before them appeared their teacher, Miss Lily.
Oh, but now she was Princess Lily, a Princess of Calvary!
The girls could not believe their eyes. They awkwardly tried
to curtsy. Princess Lily smiled as she hugged them.

"I've been eagerly waiting for you to arrive," said Princess Lily.
"I've planned a wonderful day of surprises, too. So let's hurry.
I can't wait to show you the Castle of Calvary."

Princess Lily took the girls through many rooms of the castle.
Every room was full of wonder and amazement. At last, they
entered the royal banquet hall. The table had been beautifully
set for their tea party. On top of a delicate pink tablecloth
were five tea cups. Each one was different from the other.
Every tea cup was a different color, shape and size.
The yummiest looking tea cakes made in the shape of tiaras
decorated each jeweled plate. And right in the center of
the table sat the prettiest pink flowers
Caroline had ever seen.

" 'In my Father's house are many rooms; if it were not so, I would have told you. I am going there to prepare a place for you.' "
John 14:2

Princess Lily said, "I'm very glad you came.
You were invited here today because you've wanted
to become real princesses."

"You mean this isn't a surprise for my birthday?" fussed Prissy Crissy.

"I'm afraid not," Princess Lily replied. "We're here to have fun and learn
about God's truth for princesses." She poured each girl some pink princess
tea. "Can anyone tell me what it means to be a real princess?" she asked.

"That's easy-smeasy!" cried Prissy Crissy. "A real princess belongs to a
royal family, and her parents are the king and queen of the universe! And
a real princess has a gazillion maids who do whatever she wants." Prissy
Crissy looked over her shoulder at Caroline to see if she was listening.

"Well, that's not completely correct," Princess Lily said sweetly.
"A real prin…"

"Oh, I know! I know!" interrupted Prissy Crissy.
"A real princess wears a pretty crown and
beautiful dresses. And she has a beautiful
princess face just like me!"

"Yes, you do have a lovely face," Princess Lily replied.
"But your face, your hair, and pretty dresses don't make
you a real princess. Look at the flowers on our table.
These pink flowers are pretty now, but in a few days they won't
be beautiful anymore. Outside beauty always fades away.
But real, lasting beauty comes from inside your heart."

Princess Lily paused and smiled. "You see, a real princess has a heart
full of love for her King, and that is what makes her beautiful.
The King doesn't care about your face, your hair, or your dresses.
He already thinks you're beautiful. What truly pleases Him is a heart
that loves others. Even though fancy dresses are fun to wear,
they can never make you a real princess."

"I don't believe it!" shouted Prissy Crissy. "You can't mean
that the way I treat other people is more important
than the pretty dresses I wear!"

"Actually that is true," Princess Lily responded.
"A real princess has a heart full of love.
But Caroline, do you know what it
means to be a real princess?"

"Well, a real princess has to be a
king's daughter, right?" Caroline answered softly.
She looked down, and oh, how she hoped she was wrong.

"That is absolutely right!" cried Princess Lily. "You see, to be
a real princess; your father not only has to be a king,
but He has to be the King of Kings and Lord of Lords!"

"Then Prissy Crissy was right!" cried Caroline. "I don't have a father!
How can I ever become a real princess?"

"Oh, Caroline! Is that why you've been so sad? You've been
thinking about your earthly father. But I've been talking about your
heavenly Father," Princess Lily said softly.

"My heavenly Father?" Caroline asked.

"Do you remember when you first believed that Jesus died on the cross
for all the bad things you've done?" asked Princess Lily. Caroline
nodded as Princess Lily continued, "You became a real princess
the moment you prayed and asked Jesus to live in your heart.
And since He is the King of Kings and you are
His daughter, that makes you His…"

" 'I will be a Father to you, and you will be my sons and daughters, says the Lord Almighty.' " 2 Corinthians 6:18

"Princess? Do you mean it? Me? A real princess?" Caroline cried. She could hardly believe her ears! She had been a real princess all along. She just hadn't known it. She hadn't understood that with Jesus in her heart she was a daughter of the King of Kings ~ a real princess! But then, Caroline stopped. She didn't know how to act or think like a real princess. "Oh, Princess Lily," Caroline said quickly. "I want to know everything about who I am to Jesus. I want to be the princess He wants me to be!"

"He has taken me to the banquet hall, and his banner over me is love." Song of Songs 2:4

Holy to the Lord

Holy to the Lord

"Sweet Caroline, this is cause for a Royal Celebration! Because you are a daughter of the King and finally understand that truth, I would like to present you with your very own Truth Tiara," said Princess Lily proudly. The sound of trumpets filled the room as Constant appeared carrying a sparkling crown. Princess Lily gently placed the Truth Tiara on Caroline's head.

"This tiara is more beautiful than I could have ever dreamed!" exclaimed Caroline.

All the girls were excited about Caroline's new crown. All of them except Prissy Crissy. She was upset because she didn't have a Truth Tiara for herself. But before she could complain...

...it was time for the girls to go home. Constant announced that the carriage had arrived. So Princess Lily and the girls hugged and sadly said good-bye.

As the girls walked out through the great hall, Caroline asked, "Princess Lily? Can I keep my Truth Tiara?"

"Absolutely!" replied Princess Lily. The girls climbed into the carriage. "May you keep it to remind you that you are a real princess of the King of Kings."

Suddenly, Caroline awoke. She heard her grandmother singing, "Wake up my sleepy head! It's time for my princess to get out of bed."

And Caroline sat straight up and joyfully shouted…

"I really am a princess!"

Holy to the Lord

How do I become a Daughter of the King?

To become a daughter of the King you have to believe Jesus died on the cross for your sins, and that He was raised again three days later. Sins are the bad things we do such as lying, disobeying and being selfish.

"For God so loved the world that he gave his one and only Son, that whoever believes in him shall not perish but have eternal life." ~ John 3:16

Then you pray and ask Jesus into your heart, not just so you can be a real princess, but because you love Him and believe He died for you.

"…if you confess with your mouth, 'Jesus is Lord,' and believe in your heart that God raised him from the dead, you will be saved." ~ Romans 10:9

The moment you pray and ask Jesus into your heart as Lord and Savior you become a real princess!

" 'I will be a Father to you, and you will be my sons and daughters, says the Lord Almighty.' " ~ 2 Corinthians 6:18

You will also live happily-ever-after in eternity with Jesus one day.

"For the wages of sin is death, but the gift of God is eternal life in Christ Jesus our Lord." ~ Romans 6:23

A Princess Prayer

Dear Jesus, I know that I have sin in my life. I know I can't get rid of my sin by doing good things. I know I need you to take my sin away. I believe you died on the cross for my sins and that you rose again. Please come and live in my heart. I want you to be Lord of my life. Thank you Jesus that I am now a daughter of the King of Kings!

Hear ye! Hear ye! Hear ye!

Holy to
the Lord

Let it be known throughout the land.

Princess _____ is now part of God's royal plan!

For she prayed and asked Jesus into her heart,

where He will live forever and never depart.

She also believes He died on the cross for her sins,

and then three days later He arose again.

The date of her decision _____ whereupon the angels did sing,

was the day they celebrated her

becoming a daughter of the King!

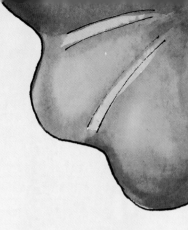

Holy to the Lord

"The king is enthralled by your beauty; honor him, for he is your lord." Psalm 45:11